D1391460

THE SMALL MIRACLE

With drawings by
EDGAR NORFIELD

Also by Paul Gallico

THE SNOW GOOSE

PAUL GALLICO

The Small Miracle

GUILD PUBLISHING LONDON

This edition first published 1985 by
Book Club Associates
by arrangement with Michael Joseph Ltd.
© 1951 by Paul Gallico

Printed and bound in Great Britain by
Blantyre Printing Ltd., London and Glasgow

To
ST FRANCIS
a man among
saints

The beautiful setting of Assisi is clearly essential for the purposes of this story. But the characters exist only in the imagination of the author and are not based upon any real persons. They are delineated as they are for purely literary reasons.

Approaching Assisi via the chalky, dusty road that twists its way up Monte Subasio, now revealing, now concealing the exquisite little town, as it winds its way through olive and cypress groves, you eventually reach a division where your choice lies between an upper and a lower route.

If you select the latter, you soon find yourself entering Assisi through the twelfth-century archway of the denticulated door of St. Francis. But if, seduced by the clear air, the wish to mount even closer to the canopy of blue Italian sky and expose still more of the delectable view of the rich Umbrian valley below, you choose the upper way, you and your vehicle eventually become inextricably entangled in the welter of humanity, oxen, goats, bawling calves, mules, fowl, children, pigs, booths and carts gathered at the market place outside the walls.

It is here you would be most likely to encounter Pepino, with his donkey Violetta, hard at work, turning his hand to anything whereby a small boy and a strong, willing beast of burden could win for themselves the crumpled ten and twenty lira notes needed to buy food and pay for lodging in the barn of Niccolo the stableman.

Pepino and Violetta were everything to each other. They were a familiar sight about Assisi and its immediate environs—the thin brown boy, ragged and barefooted, with the enormous dark eyes, large ears, and close-cropped, upstanding hair, and the dust-coloured little donkey with the Mona Lisa smile.

Pepino was ten years old and an orphan, his father, mother and near relatives having been killed

in the war. In self-reliance, wisdom and demeanour he was, of course, much older, a circumstance aided by his independence, for Pepino was an unusual orphan in that having a heritage he need rely on no one. Pepino's heritage was Violetta.

She was a good, useful and docile donkey, alike as any other with friendly, gentle eyes, soft taupe-coloured muzzle, and long, pointed brown ears, with one exception that distinguished her. Violetta had a curious expression about the corners of her mouth, as though she were smiling gently over something that amused or pleased her. Thus, no matter what kind of work, or how much she was asked to do, she always appeared to be performing it with a smile of quiet satisfaction. The combination of Pepino's dark lustrous eyes and Violetta's smile was so harmonious that people favoured them and they were able not only to earn enough for their keep but, aided and advised by Father Damico, the priest of their parish, to save a little as well.

There were all kinds of things they could do—carry loads of wood or water, deliver purchases carried in the panniers that thumped against Violetta's sides, hire out to help pull a cart mired in the mud, aid in the olive harvest, and even, occasionally, help some citizen who was too encumbered with wine to reach his home on foot, by means of a four-footed taxi with Pepino walking beside to see that the drunkard did not fall off.

But this was not the only reason for the love that existed between boy and donkey, for Violetta was more than just the means of his livelihood. She was mother to him, and father, brother, playmate, companion, and comfort. At night, in the straw of Niccolo's stable, Pepino slept curled up close to her when it was cold, his head pillowed on her neck.

Since the mountainside was a rough world for a small boy, he was sometimes beaten or injured, and then he could creep to her for comfort and Violetta would gently nuzzle his bruises. When there was joy in his heart, he shouted songs into her waving ears; when he was lonely and hurt, he could lean his head against her soft, warm flank and cry out his tears.

On his part, he fed her, watered her, searched her for ticks and parasites, picked stones from her hoofs, scratched and groomed and curried her, lavished affection on her, particularly when they were alone, while in public he never beat her with the donkey stick more than was necessary. For this treatment Violetta made a god of Pepino, and repaid him with loyalty, obedience and affection.

Thus, when one day in the early spring Violetta fell ill, it was the most serious thing that had ever happened to Pepino. It began first with an unusual lethargy that would respond neither to stick nor caresses, nor the young, strident voice urging her on. Later Pepino observed other symptoms and a visible loss of weight. Her ribs, once so well padded, began to show through her sides. But most distressing, either through a change in the conformation of her head, due to growing thinner, or because of the distress of the illness, Violetta lost her enchanting and lovable smile.

Drawing upon his carefully hoarded reserves of lira notes and parting with several of the impressive denomination of a hundred, Pepino called in Dr. Bartoli, the vet.

The vet. examined her in good faith, dosed her, and tried his best; but she did not improve and, instead, continued to lose weight and grow weaker. He hummed and hawed then and said, 'Well, now, it is hard to say. It might be one thing, such as the bite of a fly new to this district, or another, such as a germ settling in the intestine.' Either way, how could one tell? There had been a similar case in Foligno and another in a far-away town. He recommended resting the beast and feeding her lightly. If the illness passed from her and God willed, she might live. Otherwise, she would surely die and there would be an end to her suffering.

After he had gone away, Pepino put his cropped head on Violetta's heaving flank and wept unrestrainedly. But then, when the storm, induced by the fear of losing his only companion in the world, had subsided, he knew what he must do. If there was no help for Violetta on earth, the appeal must be registered above. His plan was nothing less than to take Violetta into the crypt beneath the lower church of the Basilica of St. Francis, where rested the remains of the Saint who had so dearly loved God's creations, including all the feathered and the four-footed brothers and sisters who served Him. There he would beg St. Francis to heal her. Pepino had no doubt that the Saint would do so when he saw Violetta.

These things Pepino knew from Father Damico, who had a way of talking about St. Francis as though he were a living person who might still be encountered in his frayed cowl, bound with a hemp cord at the middle, merely by turning a corner of the Main Square in Assisi or by walking down one of the narrow, cobbled streets.

And besides, there was a precedent. Giani, his friend, the son of Niccolo the stableman, had taken his sick kitten into the crypt and asked St. Francis to heal her, and the cat had got well—at least half well, anyway, for her hind legs still dragged a little; but at least she had not died. Pepino felt that if Violetta were to die, it would be the end of everything for him.

Thereupon, with considerable difficulty, he persuaded the sick and shaky donkey to rise, and with urgings and caresses and minimum use of the stick drove her through the crooked streets of Assisi and up the hill to the Basilica of St. Francis. At the beautiful twin portal of the lower church he respectfully asked Fra Bernard, who was on duty there, for permission to take Violetta down to St. Francis, so that she might be made well again.

Fra Bernard was a new monk, and, calling Pepino a young and impious scoundrel, ordered him and his donkey to be off. It was strictly forbidden to bring livestock into the church, and even to think of taking an ass into the crypt of St. Francis was a

desecration. And besides, how did he imagine she
would get down there when the narrow, winding
staircase was barely wide enough to accommodate
humans in single file, much less four-footed
animals? Pepino must be a fool as well as a shiftless
rascal.

As ordered, Pepino retreated from the portal, his
arm about Violetta's neck, and bethought himself
of what he must do next to succeed in his purpose,
for while he was disappointed at the rebuff he had
received, he was not at all discouraged.

Despite the tragedy that had struck Pepino's early
life and robbed him of his family, he really con-
sidered himself a most fortunate boy, compared
with many, since he had acquired not only a
heritage to aid him in earning a living but also an
important precept by which to live.

This maxim, the golden key to success, had been
left with Pepino, together with bars of chocolate,
chewing gum, peanut brittle, soap, and other

delights, by a corporal in the United States Army who had, in the six months he had been stationed in the vicinity of Assisi, been Pepino's demigod and hero. His name was Francis Xavier O'Halloran, and what he told Pepino before he departed out of his life for ever was, 'If you want to get ahead in this world, kid, don't never take no for an answer. Get it?' Pepino never forgot this important advice.

He thought now that his next step was clear; nevertheless, he went first to his friend and adviser, Father Damico, for confirmation.

Father Damico, who had a broad head, lustrous eyes, and shoulders shaped as though they had been especially designed to support the burdens laid upon them by his parishioners, said, 'You are within your rights, my son, in taking your request to the lay Supervisor and it lies within his power to grant or refuse it.'

There was no malice in the encouragement he thus

gave Pepino, but it was also true that he was not loath to see the Supervisor brought face to face with an example of pure and innocent faith. For in his private opinion that worthy man was too much concerned with the twin churches that formed the Basilica and the crypt as a tourist attraction. He, Father Damico, could not see why the child should not have his wish, but, of course, it was out of his jurisdiction. He was, however, curious about how the Supervisor would react, even though he thought he knew in advance.

However, he did not impart his fears to Pepino and merely called after him as he was leaving, 'And if the little one cannot be got in from above, there is another entrance from below, through the old church, only it has been walled up for a hundred years. But it could be opened. You might remind the Supervisor when you see him. He knows where it is.'

Pepino thanked him and went back alone to the

Basilica and the monastery attached to it and asked permission to see the Supervisor.

This personage was an accessible man, and even though he was engaged in a conversation with the Bishop, he sent for Pepino, who walked into the cloister gardens where he waited respectfully for the two great men to finish.

The two dignitaries were walking up and down, and Pepino wished it were the Bishop who was to say yea or nay to his request, as he looked the kindlier of the two, the Supervisor appearing to have more the expression of a merchant. The boy pricked up his ears, because, as it happened, so they were speaking of St. Francis, and the Bishop was just remarking with a sigh, 'He has been gone too long from this earth. The lesson of his life is plain to all who can read. But who in these times will pause to do so?'

The Supervisor said, 'His tomb in the crypt attracts many to Assisi. But in a Holy Year, relics are even better. If we but had the tongue of the Saint, or a lock of his hair, or a fingernail.'

The Bishop had a far-away look in his eyes, and he was shaking his head gently. 'It is a message we are in need of, my dear Supervisor, a message from a great heart that would speak to us across the gap of seven centuries to remind us of The Way.' And here he paused and coughed, for he was a polite man and noticed that Pepino was waiting.

The Supervisor turned also and said, 'Ah yes, my son, what is it that I can do for you?'

Pepino said, 'Please, sir, my donkey Violetta is very sick. The Doctor Bartoli has said he can do nothing more and perhaps she will die. Please, I would like permission to take her into the tomb of Saint Francis and ask him to cure her. He loved all animals, and particularly little donkeys. I am sure he will make her well.'

The Supervisor looked shocked. 'A donkey. In

the crypt. However did you come to that idea?'

Pepino explained about Giani and his sick kitten, while the Bishop turned away to hide a smile.

But the Supervisor was not smiling. He asked, 'How did this Giani succeed in smuggling a kitten into the tomb?'

Since it was all over, Pepino saw no reason for not telling, and replied,

'Under his coat, sir.'

The Supervisor made a mental note to warn the brothers to keep a sharper eye out for small boys or other persons with suspicious - looking lumps under their outer clothing.

'Of course we can have no such goings on,' he said. 'The next thing you know, everyone would be coming, bringing a sick dog, or an ox, or a goat, or even a pig. And then where should we end up? A veritable sty.'

'But, sir,' Pepino pleaded, 'no one need know. We would come and go so very quickly.'

The Supervisor's mind played. There was something touching about the boy—the bullet head, the enormous eyes, the jug-handle ears. And yet, what if he permitted it and the donkey then died, as seemed most likely if Dr. Bartoli had said there was no further hope? Word was sure to get about, and the shrine would suffer from it. He wondered what the Bishop was thinking and how *he* would solve the problem.

He equivocated: 'And besides, even if we were to allow it, you would never be able to get your donkey around the turn at the bottom of the stairs. So, you see, it is quite impossible.'

'But there is another entrance,' Pepino said. 'From the old church. It has not been used for a long time, but it could be opened just this once—couldn't it?'

The Supervisor was indignant. 'What are you saying—destroy church property? The entrance has been walled up for over a century, ever since the new crypt was built.'

The Bishop thought he saw a way out and said gently to the boy, 'Why do you not go home and pray to Saint Francis to assist you? If you open your heart to him and have faith, he will surely hear you.'

'But it wouldn't be the same,' Pepino cried, and his voice was shaking with the sobs that wanted to come. 'I must take her where Saint Francis can see her. She isn't like any other old donkey—Violetta has the sweetest smile. She does not smile any more since she has been so ill. But perhaps she would, just once more for Saint Francis. And when he saw it he would not be able to resist her, and he would make her well. I know he would!'

The Supervisor knew his ground now. He said, 'I am sorry, my son, but the answer is no.'

But even through his despair and the bitter tears he shed as he went away, Pepino knew that if Violetta was to live he must not take no for an answer.

'Who is there, then?' Pepino asked of Father Damico later. 'Who is above the Supervisor and my lord the Bishop who might tell them to let me take Violetta into the crypt?'

Father Damico's stomach felt cold as he thought of the dizzying hierarchy between Assisi and Rome. Nevertheless, he explained as best he could, concluding with, 'And at the top is His Holiness, the Pope himself. Surely his heart would be touched by what has happened if you were able to tell him, for he is a great and good man. But he is busy with important weighty affairs, Pepino, and it would be impossible for him to see you.'

Pepino went back to Niccolo's stable, where he ministered to Violetta, fed and watered her and rubbed her muzzle a hundred times. Then he withdrew his money from the stone jar buried under the straw and counted it. He had almost three hundred lire. A hundred of it he set aside and promised to his friend Giani if he would look after Violetta, while Pepino was gone, as if she were his own. Then he patted her once more, brushed away the tears that had started again at the sight of how thin she was, put on his jacket, and went out on the high road, where, using his thumb as he had learned from Corporal Francis Xavier O'Halloran, he got a lift in a lorry going to Foligno and the main road. He was on his way to Rome to see the Holy Father.

Never had any small boy looked quite so infinitesimal and forlorn as Pepino standing in the boundless and almost deserted, since it was early in the morning, St. Peter's Square. Everything towered over him—the massive dome of St. Peter's, the obelisk of Caligula, the Bernini colonnades. Everything contrived to make him look pinched and miserable in his bare feet, torn trousers, and ragged jacket. Never was a boy more overpowered, lonely, and frightened, or carried a greater burden of unhappiness in his heart.

For now that he was at last in Rome, the gigantic proportions of the buildings and monuments, their

awe and majesty, began to sap his courage, and he seemed to have a glimpse into the utter futility and hopelessness of his mission. And then there would arise in his mind a picture of the sad little donkey who did not smile any more, her heaving flanks and clouded eyes, and who would surely die unless he could find help for her. It was thoughts like these that enabled him finally to cross the piazza and timidly approach one of the smaller side entrances to the Vatican.

The Swiss guard, in his slashed red, yellow, and blue uniform, with his long halberd, looked enormous and forbidding. Nevertheless, Pepino edged up to him and said, 'Please, will you take me to see the Pope? I wish to speak to him about my donkey Violetta, who is very ill and may die unless the Pope will help me.'

The guard smiled, not unkindly, for he was used to these ignorant and innocent requests, and the fact that it came from a dirty, ragged little boy, with

eyes like ink pools and a round head from which the
ears stood out like the handles on a cream jug, made
it all the more harmless. But, nevertheless, he was
shaking his head as he smiled, and then said that His
Holiness was a very busy man and could not be seen.
And the guard grounded his halberd with a thud
and let it fall slantwise across the door to show that
he meant business.

Pepino backed away. What good was his precept
in the face of such power and majesty? And yet the
memory of what Corporal O'Halloran had said told
him that he must return to the Vatican yet once
again.

At the side of the piazza he saw an old woman
sitting under an umbrella, selling little bouquets and
nosegays of spring flowers—daffodils and jonquils,
snowdrops and white narcissus, Parma violets and
lilies of the valley, vari-coloured carnations, pansies,
and tiny sweetheart roses. Some of the people
visiting St. Peter's liked to place these on the altar

of their favourite saint. The flowers were crisp and fresh from the market, and many of them had glistening drops of water still clinging to their petals.

Looking at them made Pepino think of home and Father Damico and what he had said of the love St. Francis had for flowers. Father Damico had the gift of making everything he thought and said sound like poetry. And Pepino came to the conclusion that if St. Francis, who had been a holy man, had been so fond of flowers, perhaps the Pope, who according to his position was even holier, would love them, too.

For fifty lire he bought a tiny bouquet in which a spray of lilies of the valley rose from a bed of dark violets and small red roses crowded next to yellow pansies all tied about with leaf and feather fern and paper lace.

From a stall where postcards and souvenirs were sold, he begged pencil and paper, and laboriously composed a note:

Dear and most sacred Holy Father: These flowers are for you. Please let me see you and tell you about my donkey Violetta who is dying, and they will not let me take her to see Saint Francis so that he may cure her. I live in the town of Assisi, but I have come all the way here to see you.

Your loving Pepino.

Thereupon, he returned to the door, placed the bouquet and the note in the hand of the Swiss guard, and begged, 'Please take these up to the Pope. I am sure he will see me when he receives the flowers and reads what I have written.'

The guard had not expected this. The child and the flowers had suddenly placed him in a dilemma from which he could not extricate himself in the presence of those large and trusting eyes. However, he was not without experience in handling such matters. He had only to place a colleague at his post, go to the Guard Room, throw the flowers and the note into the wastepaper basket, absent himself for a sufficient length of time, and then return to tell the boy that His Holiness thanked him for the gift of the flowers and regretted that press of important business made it impossible for him to grant him an audience.

This little subterfuge the guard put into motion at once; but when he came to completing the next-to-last act in it, he found to his amazement that somehow he could not bring himself to do it. There was the wastepaper basket, yawning to receive the offering, but the little nosegay seemed to be glued to his fingers. How gay, sweet, and cool the flowers were. What thoughts they brought to his mind of spring in the green valleys of his far-off canton of Luzern. He saw again the snow-capped mountains of his youth, the little gingerbread houses, the grey, soft-eyed cattle grazing in the blossom-carpeted meadows, and he heard the heart-warming tinkling of their bells.

Dazed by what had happened to him, he left the Guard Room and wandered through the corridors, for he did not know where to go or what to do with his burden. He was eventually encountered by a busy little Monsignor, one of the vast army of clerks and secretaries employed in the Vatican, who paused, astonished at the sight of the burly guard helplessly contemplating a tiny posy.

And thus occurred the minor miracle whereby Pepino's plea and offering crossed the boundary in the palace that divided the mundane from the spiritual, the lay from the ecclesiastical.

For to the great relief of the guard, the Monsignor took over the burning articles that he had been unable to relinquish; and this priest they touched, too, as it is the peculiar power of flowers that while they are universal and spread their species over the world, they invoke in each beholder the dearest and most cherished memories.

In this manner, the little bouquet passed on and upward from hand to hand, pausing briefly in the possession of the clerk of the Apostolic Chamber, the Privy Almoner, the Papal Sacristan, the Master of the Sacred Palaces, the Papal Chamberlain. The dew vanished from the flowers; they began to lose their freshness and to wilt, passing from hand to hand. And yet they retained their magic, the message of love and memories that rendered it impossible for any of these intermediaries to dispose of them.

Eventually, then, they were deposited with the missive that accompanied them on the desk of the man for whom they had been destined. He read the note and then sat there silently contemplating the blossoms. He closed his eyes for a moment, the better to entertain the picture that arose in his mind of himself as a small Roman boy taken on a Sunday into the Alban Hills, where for the first time he saw violets growing wild.

When he opened his eyes at last, he said to his
secretary, 'Let the child be brought here. I will see
him.'

Thus it was that Pepino at last came into the
presence of the Pope, seated at his desk in his
office. Perched on the edge of a chair next to
him, Pepino told the whole story about Violetta,
his need to take her into the tomb of St. Francis,
about the Supervisor who was preventing him,
and all about Father Damico, too, and the
second entrance
to the crypt,
Violetta's smile,
and his love
for her—every-
thing, in fact,
that was in
his heart and
that now
poured forth to

the sympathetic man sitting quietly behind the desk.

And when, at the end of half an hour, he was ushered from the presence, he was quite sure he was the happiest boy in the world. For he had not only the blessing of the Pope, but also, under his jacket, two letters, one addressed to the lay Supervisor of the Monastery of Assisi and the other to Father Damico. No longer did he feel small and over-whelmed when he stepped out on to the square again past the astonished but delighted Swiss guard. He felt as though he could give one leap and a bound and fly back to his Violetta's side.

Nevertheless, he had to give heed to the more practical side of transportation. He enquired his way to a bus that took him to where the Via Flaminia became a country road stretching to the north, then plied his thumb backed by his eloquent eyes, and before nightfall of that day, with good luck, was home in Assisi.

After a visit to Violetta had assured him that she had been well looked after and at least was no worse than she had been before his departure, Pepino proudly went to Father Damico and presented his letters as he had been instructed to do.

The Father fingered the envelope for the Supervisor and then, with a great surge of warmth and happiness, read the one addressed to himself. He said to Pepino, 'To-morrow we will take the Supervisor's letter to him. He will summon masons and the old door will be broken down and you will be able to take Violetta into the tomb and pray there for her recovery. The Pope himself has approved it.'

The Pope, of course, had not written the letters personally. They had been composed with considerable delight and satisfaction by the Cardinal-Secretary, backed by Papal authority, who said in his missive to Father Damico:

Surely the Supervisor must know that in his lifetime the blessed Saint Francis was accompanied to chapel by a little lamb that used to follow him about Assisi. Is an asinus *any less created by God because his coat is rougher and his ears longer?*

And he wrote also of another matter, which Father Damico imparted to Pepino in his own way.

He said, 'Pepino, there is something you must understand before we go to see the Abbot. It is your hope that because of your faith in St. Francis he will help you and heal your donkey. But had you thought, perhaps, that he who dearly cared for all of God's creatures might come to love Violetta so greatly that he would wish to have her at his side in Eternity?'

A cold terror gripped Pepino as he listened. He managed to say, 'No, Father, I had not thought——'

The priest continued: 'Will you go to the crypt only to ask, Pepino, or will you also, if necessary, be prepared to give?'

Everything in Pepino cried out against the possibility of losing Violetta, even to someone as beloved as St. Francis. Yet when he raised his stricken face and looked into the lustrous eyes of Father  Damico, there was something in their depths that gave him the courage to whisper, 'I will give—if I must. But, oh, I hope he will let her stay with me just a little longer.'

The clink of the stone-mason's pick rang again and again through the vaulted chamber of the lower church, where the walled-up door of the passageway leading to the crypt was being removed. Nearby waited

the Supervisor and his friend the Bishop, Father
Damico, and Pepino, large-eyed, pale, and silent.
The boy kept his arms about the neck of Violetta
and his face pressed to hers. The little donkey was
very shaky on her legs and could barely stand.

The Supervisor watched humbly and impassively
while broken bricks and clods of mortar fell as the
breach widened and the freed current of air from the
passage swirled the plaster dust in clouds. He was a
just man for all his weakness, and had invited the
Bishop to witness his rebuke.

A portion of the wall proved obstinate. The
mason attacked the archway at the side to weaken
its support. Then the loosened masonry began to
tumble again. A narrow passageway was effected,
and through the opening they could see the distant
flicker of the candles placed at the altar wherein
rested the remains of St. Francis.

Pepino stirred towards the opening. Or was it
Violetta who had moved nervously, frightened by

the unaccustomed place and noises? Father Damico said, 'Wait,' and Pepino held her; but the donkey's uncertain feet slipped on the rubble and then lashed out in panic, striking the side of the archway where it had been weakened. A brick fell out. A crack appeared.

Father Damico leaped and pulled boy and animal out of the way as, with a roar, the side of the arch collapsed, laying bare a piece of the old wall and the hollow behind it before everything vanished in a cloud of dust.

But when the dust settled, the Bishop, his eyes starting from his head, was pointing to something that rested in a niche of the hollow just revealed. It was a small, grey, leaden box. Even from there they could see the year 1226, when St. Francis died, engraved on the side, and the large initial 'F.'

The Bishop's breath came out like a sigh. 'Ah, could it be? The legacy of Saint Francis! Fra Leo mentions it. It was hidden away centuries ago, and no one had ever been able to find it since.'

The Supervisor said hoarsely, 'The contents! Let us see what is inside—it may be valuable!'

The Bishop hesitated. 'Perhaps we had best wait. For this is in itself a miracle, this finding.'

But Father Damico, who was a poet and to whom St. Francis was a living spirit, cried, 'Open it, I beg of you! All who are here are humble. Surely Heaven's plan has guided us to it.'

The Abbot held the lantern. The mason with his careful, honest workman's hands deftly loosed the bindings and pried the lid of the airtight box. It opened with an ancient creaking of its hinge and revealed what had been placed there more than seven centuries before.

There was a piece of hempen cord, knotted as though, perhaps, once it had been worn about the waist. Caught in the knot, as fresh as though it had grown but yesterday, was a single sprig of wheat.

Dried and preserved, there lay, too, the stem and starry flower of a mountain primrose and, next to it, one downy feather from a tiny meadow bird.

Silently the men stared at these objects from the past to try to read their meaning, and Father Damico wept, for to him they brought the vivid figure of the Saint, half-blinded, worn and fragile, the cord knotted at his waist, singing, striding through a field of wheat. The flower might have been the first discovered by him after a winter's snow, and addressed as 'Sister Cowslip,' and praised for her tenderness and beauty. As though he were transported there, Father Damico saw the little field bird fly trustingly to Francis' shoulder and chirrup and nestle there and leave a feather in his hand. His heart was so full he thought he could not bear it.

The Bishop, too, was close to tears as, in his own way, he interpreted what they had found. 'Ah, what could be clearer than the message of the Saint? Poverty, love, and faith. This is his bequest to all of us.'

Pepino said, 'Please, lords and sirs, may Violetta and I go into the crypt now?'

They had forgotten him. Now they started up from their contemplation of the touching relics.

Father Damico cleared the tears from his eyes. The doorway was freed now, and there was room for boy and donkey to pass. 'Ah, yes,' he said. 'Yes, Pepino. You may enter now. And may God go with you.'

The hoofs of the donkey went sharply *clip-clop*, *clip-clop* on the ancient flagging of the passageway. Pepino did not support her now, but walked beside, hand just resting lightly and lovingly on her neck. His round, cropped head with the outstanding ears was held high, and his shoulders were bravely squared.

And to Father Damico it seemed, as they passed,

whether because of the uneven light and the dancing shadows, or because he wished it so, that the ghost, the merest wisp, the barest suspicion of a smile had returned to the mouth of Violetta.

Thus the watchers saw boy and donkey silhouetted against the flickering oil lamps and altar candles of the crypt as they went forward to complete their pilgrimage of faith.